The Plot
Against
Heaven

The Plot Against Heaven

By

Mark Kirkbride

For Denise

With thanks for all you do for mum.
From

Mark Kirkbride

Omnium Gatherum
Los Angeles

By the Same Author

Game Changers of the Apocalypse

Satan's Fan Club

I'm standing in the office of the Superbeing watching the towers of heaven fall, knowing that it's all my fault.

Jets dash across the sky, missiles streaking.

I never intended to get involved in the eternal struggle between heaven and hell but events had other plans for me. I opened the gate that let the forces of hell in, turned the cold war hot.

A helicopter passes over the city. Rockets shoot from pods slung either side of the airframe.

The building shudders. An alarm blares.

Smoke darkens another clutch of towers.

"Repair to the bunkers," a voice repeats over the PA.

Behind me, through the doorway, bodies lie as if in mimicry of the postures in which they fell.

I'm still staring out of the floor-to-ceiling window.

A bug-headed helicopter heads this way.

"You know what to do," says a voice in my ear.

Yeah, to stop the war I have to commit an act that would make me the enemy of heaven and earth, if I'm not already.

The thing is, my wife's down there, in all that chaos.

Some borders you can cross but can you get back?

Chapter 1

A Glimpse of God

"Dear Sir, I have a complaint."

That's how I began the message I sent. When I didn't receive anything by way of a reply, I tried to call. "He's on the other line," His assistant told me. "You'll have to hold." I held, and held. And held. Eventually the line beeped and flatlined. Which only confirmed that this needed to be done in person. I made an appointment and here I am on my way to meet Him, to meet God.

The passenger compartment of the car is like a cab's. It's separated from the front by a tinted partition. I can see the back of my driver's head and he can see me in his rear-view mirror. Not that either of us talk. Both of us know the vehicle could be bugged.

The silver car bowls along the wide, tree-lined boulevard. To either side, gated white properties hide behind walls.

Digital billboards at the side of the road carry messages such as "Assume the enemy is listening", "If you spot suspicious activity, call the Guardians immediately" and—scrolling—"Looking forward to welcoming friends and relations? Treat all new arrivals with utmost caution. It's possible they may have been turned since you last saw them."

The houses fall away to the left and, behind a high chain-wire perimeter fence, this side of a huge expanse of mostly grassed land with hangars on the far side, six gleaming fighter jets line up to take off. The first turns onto the runway and, with its engine roaring, flames shooting out of the back, hurtles up the strip of Tarmac, eases into the air, climbs steeply and banks sharply.

Already turning, the next sets off after it.

A little further on, on the other side of the road, a pair of tanks maneuver up a track. A head with a beret on it poking out of the top of the rear tank sways with each twitch of the turret. A long droopy antenna bobs at the back.

An armored helicopter thumps by not much higher than the rooftops.

When did heaven become a militarized zone?

Sirens rise and dip and rise again behind us, overlapping. Are we speeding?

The sirens loop louder, closer.

My driver slows down and moves over to hug the curb. A deep rumble gathers pace behind us before separating out into two competing whines as a policeman on a motorcycle accelerates past followed by another. Blue lights on poles at the back of each bike revolve like neutron stars.

They pull up at a crossroads ahead and, one blocking the lane to join or cross the dual carriageway from the nearside, the other at a 45-degree angle across the far side, both raise white-gloved hands to stop the traffic from every direction except ours.

I turn around to peer through the rear window at a white limousine flanked by two outriders looming in the outside lane.

I turn back to try to catch them as they pass us but they sweep by too fast.

All I can make out in the limousine's rear window amid shimmer and glare—between two more outriders—is the shadow of a cranium.

Him! I'm sure it is. Who else can it be?

I sit up, tap the partition. My escort jaunts his head.

I lean closer. "Follow that limo."

As he lowers and lifts his head, acceleration presses me back into my seat.

We're still falling behind but at a decreasing rate. Most

of the other traffic peels off up ramps.

A bridge frames a red-and-white striped pole barring the road.

Damn. Checkpoint.

The limo slows ahead of us.

Catching up, we trail it under the bridge. The pole shoots up. The limo passes through. Just as suddenly, the pole descends.

I nearly slide off my seat as, braking, the car judders and rocks to a halt.

Pressing off from the partition, I sit up.

Beyond the bridge, a 15-foot-high steel fence stretches to either side with rolls of razor wire along the top.

A soldier strolls around our car with a semi-automatic that fits snugly in his arms angled at 45 degrees.

Another steps out of the booth to check the driver's permit. He hands it back, raps at my window with a black-gloved hand and peers in. He's leaning sideways with neck bent and head vertical, which, pushing an epaulette towards his ear, gives him a one-sided hunch.

Of course, he's trying to stop his cap falling off. A wire issues from one ear. Nasal hairs that need trimming vibrate with each exhalation.

When, thanks to the driver, my window whirrs down half way, I reach in my pocket.

The solider stiffens.

The faint click-click-click of a finger nestling up against a trigger.

I pull out my pass.

A clack of cleats as the soldier shuffles. He sniffs. Snatching the card, he studies it.

His face withdraws as he stands up straight and shoves his hand in through the gap.

I take the pass.

Tap-tap, on the roof, and the barrier springs upright.

My window closes and we inch forwards.

A camera twitches on the wall of the booth.

Long sleek barrels poking out from the tops of lookout towers keep up with us.

A drone hovering off to the side lurches forwards swinging on its lateral axis.

The soaring trees of a wood give way to the flat expanse of a lake.

Then I see it, beyond sculpted gardens and twice as high as neighboring towers, the skyscraper with a horizontal section cantilevering out to left and right two thirds of the way up.

A white car curves around towards the base.

It speeds down a ramp and a metal grille descends behind it.

God's in situ.

Chapter 2

An Appointment with God

Ping.

The lift door opens and, having left my driver waiting in the car downstairs, I step out into a corridor with flat wall lights, niches with lamps, carpet that registers one's footfalls with the softest of thunks and a strip of recessed ceiling lights leading the way.

The carpet's short pile gives under me in unexpected directions as I turn a corner.

Now the corridor opens out into a larger space with windows down one side. Chairs face inwards.

On the far side, a man in a dark suit sits at a desk. He's facing me. Or he would be if he wasn't angled over a terminal.

Making heavy weather of it on the carpet's stiff fibers, I head towards him.

He glances at me briefly, then carries on tapping at his keyboard, staring at his screen.

Even when I reach him, he doesn't look up.

He's wearing round glasses and has an ovoid head with short dark hair.

He sits just to one side of a set of polished doors. A "Do Not Disturb" sign hangs from one of the golden doorknobs.

I lean against the desk and rest a hand on it within his field of vision. "I'm here for my appointment."

He looks up with oversized eyes. Or maybe that's just the glasses. "Name?"

I recognize his voice. It's the assistant that took my call.

I produce my pass. "Paul Desuthe, here about Kate Desuthe."

He coughs. "Age?"

"Thirty-four."

"Occupation?"

I put the card away, clear my throat. I need answers, not more bloody questions. "Poet."

The assistant points to a row of chairs over by the window. "Take a seat."

I check my watch. I'm on time. Why do I have to wait?

Sighing through my nose, I head over to the chairs.

Leaning against the window, I stare out at the horizon, which isn't circular but, rather, truncated ahead.

What is that? Some kind of wall annexing half of heaven?

Noticing a pane in each of the three grooves of the window frame, I peer down at the landscaped grounds far below, the steel fence and, beyond, the wide road carving its way through the city, with other roads connecting it at various angles or criss-crossing via bridges with monorails above, canals below.

Closer to the base of the tower, I can see them, as He must see them, the people going about their business in Toytown.

I sit, rehearse what I'm going to say. Why let it happen? Why separate those who love each other? The nicest people get sucked out first.

My arms are folded, locked rigid. Gripping each bicep, I squeeze hard. A huge sigh heaves out of me. I glance at my watch. Where is He? I know He's here. I dig my heels into the carpet, dig my chin into my chest. I have to keep perfectly still to stop the reservoir of emotion brimming over.

A phone rings in the room behind the assistant.

No one answers from within and he doesn't stir without.

Eventually the caller hangs up.

My neck clicks as my head tilts and turns as if on ratchets. What's that? A wavy blonde hair's wreathed its way around my sleeve. How long's that been there? One of hers? A depth charge goes off in my soul, blops to the surface as a sob.

I can't see for the tears burning my eyes. I shift between rigid postures to try and appease pangs, aches.

Now I'm in the moment rather than outside it, I've a surplus of energy. My hand smacks the arm of my seat.

I snap upright. Almost before I know what I'm doing, I'm marching over to God's assistant.

I slam my hand down on his desk. He jolts back in his seat.

"He's here, I know He is. And I need to see Him." I dash around the desk.

The assistant leaps to his feet. "What? No." Suddenly he's in front of me with the palm of his hand between us. "You don't understand. Y-You can't just go in there."

I stop. "Well, fine, let me see my wife then."

His hand jerks away. He literally flinches. "You can't. You know there's no fraternization between the living and the dead."

"Well, let me see *Him* then." As I advance, he retreats.

His jumpy pupils dart all over the place. "No, no, no, you can't." He backs up towards the pair of doors with both palms up and out now. "He's..."

I barge past, grab a golden doorknob. The door's opening and I'm inside, looking around at old books on shelves and plants on tables and dark oil paintings on the walls and a cupboard door and a giant desk curving around a big black swivel chair, the desk of the all-seeing, all-powerful one, the person with dominium over life and death. On the surface of the desk sits a phone, an intercom and a terminal like the assistant's.

At the far end, a piece of machinery clanks and whirrs.

I take a closer look. Gyroscopes spin, wheels rotate, polished silver balls roll and clack. What is it? An orrery? Some souped-up Newton's cradle? The ultimate executive toy?

The desk faces a whole wall of screens, none of which are on.

The assistant left. Now he's on his way back in.

His left hand clasps his right hand, his right his left. They switch, switch again. "You shouldn't be in here."

"Where is He?" Sinking up to my soles in the carpet, I stride over to the floor-to-ceiling window.

The view has me reeling.

When did I forget how far up we are?

"For your own sake, you need to get out of here," says the assistant from behind me.

I turn to face him.

Then I have to swivel back the other way to keep up with him as he scuttles across the room to place himself between me and the window.

An alarm bleeps behind me, out in the foyer.

"What's going on?" I half turn.

A dark bar blurs above me, whacks me over the shoulder.

Crouching, I lift my arm at an angle to fend it off as it falls again. My forearm explodes with pain.

Another blow I didn't see coming catches me on the back of the head and sends me sprawling face first into the carpet at the assistant's feet. He hops out of the way.

Head humming, with a blackness behind the eyes that threatens to rise to the surface, I scrabble in the shagpile.

I'm yanked aloft with my arms out to either side and hauled towards the door by men in black. Boots clonk. Uniforms rustle. Segmented body armor starting at their knees continues as high as I can twist my neck.

"Oi! Get—" I try to wrench my arms free, without any success.

I'm being pulled in two directions, dragged in a third.

"Hey, I had an appointment," I get out.

Opening the second door to help facilitate my abduction, the assistant holds up a hand as I pass as if to say, what, "It's out of my hands," or "Talk to the hand"?

Of God?

I think I might be concussed.

Could it have been the back of the assistant's head in the limousine?

Now I know I've got concussion.

They bustle me out of the office. Carpet rushes by. I picture the tortured, winding trail my toecaps leave—evidence that I was here for however long it lasts when I'm wherever they're taking me.

The walls close in, with faces peeping from doorways, and I swear I can hear a baby bawling somewhere. What is it, Bring Your Kid to Work Day?

There're more people peeking now.

We pass a woman on the phone.

Remembering one of the signs I spotted on the way in, I wrench my head her way. "Call the Guardians!"

"We are the fucking Guardians," one of my assailants informs me.

"What?" Oh, shit...

"There's no justice in heaven or on earth," I shout over my shoulder, for the benefit of my impromptu audience. "Just negligence at best, evil at worst!"

The Guardian that spoke gives my arm an extra tug. "You can't talk like that. Not here."

"Ow," I cry, having just been stretched. I twist my head his way. "Fine, I want nothing to do with Him. I renounce such a God!"

The other leans closer in his bulletproof vest and with the dark visor down on his helmet. "Careful what you wish for, Paul."

"How do you—"

No wonder everyone's so paranoid here.

The lift yawns ahead.

"He sacrificed His only son," I continue. "Do you think He cares about us?"

We reach the lip.

"Go to hell!" says the first, and they throw me in.

The floor crashes into me.

I roll over onto my back and shuffle up against the corner so I'm only half slumped. "He let her die," I yell, rubbing one knee and an elbow. Boxy, my voice shouts back at me. "Didn't do a thing to try and stop it!"

The taciturn Guardian leans in, presses a button and hastily withdraws.

Ping.

"My wife," I yelp, as the door trundles out of its slot.

It shuts.

The lift sinks.

Breathing hard, I push off from the floor and get to my feet. What just happened? I had an appointment with God.

I kept the appointment, He did not.

The side of the lift bangs where I punch it.

My arm and shoulder remind me of their existence in a way they don't normally do, by pulsing and with strange surges of heat. The back of my head throbs and feels twice its normal size.

The numbers drop on the digital read-out. I pass the ground floor, basement, lower basement, and they keep on going, minus numbers now, faster and faster. My body plummets. My stomach tugs the other way. There's nothing to hold onto. I brace myself against the side. I lean into a corner. Soon I'm as low as before I'd been high. How deep does this shaft go? The numbers flicker and blur. I jab buttons. My stomach bobs like a helium balloon. Where's this tin can taking me? The center of the earth?

The lift creaks, groans. My stomach about-flips. It bungee-jumps to the pit of me. A lurch throws me one way, a second back the other. They keep coming and my steps zig-zag till I lose my footing and fall. Now I'm pressed flat against the floor. It presses back against me. I couldn't get up even if I wanted to.

Closing my eyes puts me back in the car in pale darkness, with English countryside backlit by the moon, as two pairs of headlights fill the windscreen side by side. Behind the wheel, Kate gasps and does the only thing she can do. Instead of rounding the bend, she carries straight on. Both sets of lights slide out of sight as we leave the road between two trees.

Summer-full, they brush us.

A bump and the airbag punches me in the face. I thought we were stopping but the nose of the car tilts downwards and we go with it. We jump in our seats. The roof knock-knock-knocks me on the head. I can't see anything.

The car slews to Kate's side. We're still bouncing. There's a creak and over we go.

Both of us are thrown all the way round, all the way round, as in some horrific fairground ride that won't stop. An empty plastic bottle keeps falling, falling, falling. We revolve around it. The roof presses in closer each time.

Finally, a grinding one way, the other, and we come to rest.

I'm down, Kate's up. She's hanging in her seat above me.

"You okay, love?" I crane upwards. "Love? You okay?"

The dashboard lights are still on. Kate's eyes are closed. Her arm's dangling next to me.

My leg's trapped and I can't get it free.

Something wet drips on my forehead.

I touch it and peer at my hand.

It's dark.

Oil?

Another drip.

I look up and, from a gash in Kate's temple, blood pours in my face.

No, no, no...

"Kate," I cried.

No, you can't.

"Kate!" I screamed.

There's a clunk, a slotting into place. My eyes are squeezed shut.

I open them.

The lift's come to rest.

Only, where?

Ping.

Chapter 3

Otherworld

Ding-ding-ding-ding-ding-ding. The door slides open and that's the first thing I hear—that and fanfares looping in and out—as I push myself off the floor and roll over onto my backside.

A woman with plum lips, smoky eyeshadow, black eyeliner and a pale foundation, somewhere in her twenties, reaches a hand in. "Paul, welcome!"

"What?" Both sides of the back of my head knock against the corner of the lift, reminding me, twice over, of its soreness.

Head, stomach and other organs jumbled up, I take her hand, get up and step out into an enormous hall lined with row upon row of blinking, warbling slot machines.

The low-level crackle like fire feeding on kindling is the banter of hundreds of men and women trying their luck, punctuated, now here, now there, with the unmistakable cascade of coins.

The young woman that greeted me wears a black blouse with frilly collar and cuffs, black jeans with diagonal slashes and chains dangling from one side of her waist. Her long straight black hair falls in her eyes with each tilt of her head.

Realizing I'm still holding her hand, I let go.

She smiles, lowers her head, raises it again. "So, anyway, welcome." She touches her breastbone through her blouse. "Gem."

"Nice to meet you." My hand hangs emptily at my side.

I should be shaking hers.

"You too." She does a little jump—"Right, let me get you where you need to be"—and turns.

Heel and sole all of a piece, about a foot thick, her boots thunk on the floor.

I set off after her down the facing aisle.

A barman with a small round tray held aloft with several, full, glasses on it beetles the other way.

I'm about to pass him when he swerves and lowers the tray to present a glass of red wine to a woman in a floral dress and green-beaded necklace who's feeding change into one of the slot machines. "Your usual, Mrs. Krahl?"

"Oh, thank you, Mike," from behind me now.

In the corresponding row on the other side of a longitudinal dividing aisle, a man in what looks like Havaianas, shorts and a blue Hawaiian-style shirt sits slumped at another slot machine with a large paper cup of chips at his side.

Even with Gem clomping on the stilts of her boots, I remain a couple of steps behind.

"Where are we going?" I call out.

She smiles over her shoulder. "Someone wants to meet you."

I walk into a stool. It clatters against a fruit machine. Fortunately, no one's on it at the time.

We emerge from the flashing, trilling forest of machines.

High rollers at tables pick up cards, lay down cards, throw dice and study the spin of wheels. All down the side of the vast hall, men and women sit at tables in eateries. Well done steak, spicy chili con carne and cheesy pizza aromas waft our way. Stairs lead up to rooms piled like a wall of safe deposit boxes.

Music throbs at the far end of the hall, where, silhouetted by colors in the cave of a dance floor, bodies move to a song from a couple of summers ago.

I catch up with Gem and walk alongside her. "I wasn't quite expecting all... all this."

She grins and indicates the exit with the flick of a purple nail.

We step out onto a wide boulevard lined with palm trees under a black, starless dome. A billion bulbs neutralize the gloom. Apart from a Gothic pile diagonally opposite, the whole place is bejeweled with light. Buildings stand refulgent in the interplay of gold and red and orange and blue. Shot through with lasers, water leaps into the air from pools. Video screens as big as billboards stand on poles or hang from the side of buildings and advertise upcoming attractions: *The Multicolored Zebra*, a hip-hop *Othello*, a game between the Flies and the Gnats. Shadowy apart from red, green and white lights, helicopters rise and sink and turn. A few buzz towers.

On the pavement below, knots of people pass: a couple glued at the hip; three women carrying long-cord-handled logoed bags that bulge with boxes; a group of men in T-shirts, shorts and trainers in full song as if on the way home from the pub or a football match.

Open rear door level with us, a black limousine purrs at the roadside.

I stop, gesture around. "What... What is this place?" After heaven's paranoid police state, it resembles nothing so much as one giant party. "It's like... It's like Las Vegas or something."

Gem laughs. "You're not the first person to say that."

"But where are we?"

She stares at me. "Oh, I think you know where you are." Stepping towards me, she touches my arm. "And I think you know who wants to meet you."

I nod, swallow. I've a feeling I do.

"Come on," she says. "He's waiting."

Chapter 4

A Warm Welcome in Hell

I stare out of the window at the view. The city is its own illuminated map, shot through with color. Rooftops tend towards darkness but roads are splashed with overlapping light, while the lights of traffic bunch red on one side of streets, white on the other. Off to the left is a lozenge of land with nothing on it, in what looks like its own patch of daylight.

I peer out, side on.

Oh... A floodlit golf course.

The grid of streets extends for miles, with blocks of darkness at the outer edges that's followed by huge tracts of nothing. Real estate yet to be earmarked for development?

A helicopter with a winking green light and a constant white one passes a couple of dozen floors below me.

I turn away from the window to the man seated, perpendicular to me, at the desk. He's got short black hair, a close-cropped black beard, and he's wearing a short-sleeved linen shirt and cream chinos.

I gesture behind me. "Amazing view."

He stretches, lowers his arms. "Not bad."

A pause.

He turns and leans his head, nods, at an angle, at a chair.

I sit down, the Devil on one side of the desk, me on the other, and my scalp slides across the top of my skull as my eyebrows jerk aloft. How to take this in?

"Glad you could join our little community." Little? Really? One of his arms hangs over the side of his chair and he flexes and unflexes the fingers at the end of it.

"Yes, it's not as I expected at all." I clear my throat. "In a good way."

"Oh? What did you expect?" He lifts a foot to rest that ankle on the opposite knee. "Some kind of penal colony maybe?"

"I suppose. Something like that." I glance around the room, at a clock with twelve hour hands, a minute hand and a second hand, all going backwards, and a painting of the man himself facing the other way.

I turn back to the original. "What do people call you here? 'Sir'?"

"'Sir'?" He laughs. "This isn't the other place, you know. Here we're all equals. Simply engaged in the pursuit of pleasure. With everything facilitated, bottom up, not imposed, top down." He winces. "I mean, who wants to live in a dictatorship with no room for dissent?"

I cup my chin. "Are you sure this isn't heaven, and that's hell?"

He throws his head back and laughs.

His laughter peters out.

A frown crosses his face. "There's a lot of... misconceptions." His ankle slips off his knee. "Let's just say the PR put out by the other side has a lot to answer for." He clasps his hands on the desk, leans forwards. "In fact, I'm trying to do something about that."

I nod, wondering if he plans the whole operation from this desk.

He looks down, up. "What's your profession?"

"Oh, me, I'm a copyrighter." I cough. "Jingles."

He pushes back from the desk. "Ah, a poet, eh?"

I shrug. "Apparently."

"We've had a lot of poets here." He runs his fingers along the edge of the desk. "They retain their innocence.

Even the ones who've gone out of their way to get their hands dirty in life and more life. And their simplicity is something we all respond to. It's an exceptionally powerful thing." His head tilts to one side. "Perhaps we can find an outlet for your talents here."

I glance at the door. "Well, I'm just passing through."

He smiles. "Passing through, eh? Well, it's always nice to meet a... guest. Perhaps you'll sign our visitors' book." He pulls a ledger out of a drawer, sets it down, spins it around, pushes it towards me and rolls his pen across the desk.

The pen falls off the edge and I catch it.

I reach for the ledger, sign my name and slide the book over to him.

He turns it around and smiles. "I like to keep a record."

His leather chair creaks as he sits back.

He raises a loafer, sets it on the desk, and does the same with the other. His arms rest on the sides of the chair with his fingers interlocked. There's a gap between his thumbs. They revolve around each other. "So I understand this is all to do with your wife?"

"Yes. A crime's been committed. A mistake at the very least. You see, it wasn't her time. It can't be. We've only been..." I swallow. The sump of grief, always brimming, is ready to slop over. I keep very still as if balancing a full pitcher on my head. "We've only been married a few mon..." My chin drops.

I continue very quietly.

I was in bed when we met.

I heard rustling and, eyes closed, turned my head towards it. "I hope they've got all of it this time."

"Oh, you're awake." It was like my own soul speaking back at me.

I opened my eyes.

One of the two curtains around my bed had been pulled

all down one side and round to the far corner, inches from the other, so I couldn't see out, but a woman stood within it at the foot of my bed. She wore scrubs and held a pen to a clipboard.

The ballpoint rolled and scratched.

In the half-light, I could see that she had wavy shoulder-length blonde hair and skin so clear as to be almost translucent.

"I am?" I said.

She stopped writing to look at me.

Shot to pieces by her eyes, set in a heart-shaped face, I couldn't stop staring. "Sure I'm not still dreaming?"

At the other end of the ward, someone snored so loudly that it woke him up. Lips smack-smack-smacked, before the snoring started up again.

The corner of my mouth snagged on a memory and my hand went up to my newly naked head.

She hooked the back of the clipboard over the bar at the foot of the bed.

"Just as I thought," she said, holding the curtain back as she shuffled round the overbed table parked there for the night. "Harmlessly delirious."

"Oh, harmless, eh?" I pushed myself up into a half sitting position. "If..." I settled back against the pillows. "When I get out of here, I'm taking you to dinner."

Her head rocked on the stem of her neck.

She paused at the gap in the curtain.

Right before she stepped through it, I heard, in a sing-song, "Okay."

"Bye, Nin. Thank you for looking after me so well. Reyna, I'm sorry for all the trouble I gave you. Monique, thank you for everything. And please thank Eric for me. You've all been brilliant."

I worked along the line near the nurses' station, just yards away from the way out, saying goodbye to the nurses on duty with hugs and handshakes. They'd stopped what they were doing in the ward and behind the desk to see me off.

Kate had her back to me. Deep in conversation with a colleague, she had her feet in the nurse's station and her head in the office behind it.

One pump, bent from the toes and lifted at the rear, pivoted this way and that.

"Sure you don't want a wheelchair?" said Monique.

"No, I'll be fine, thanks. Really." I gave a wave. "Bye, everyone."

In unison this time: "Bye, Paul."

Everyone dispersed around me and I lifted my bag by its handles, hooked the strap over my shoulder and headed towards the exit.

As I passed the desk, Kate turned and we walked out together.

I pushed the door open. She glided through. I followed.

Our paths lay at right angles—hers towards the adjacent ward, mine up the corridor.

We both shuffled to a halt.

Her skin glowed. The filaments of her hair shone. Transcendentally beautiful, feminine to her fingertips, she glanced off to one side.

I exhaled. "Thank you for getting me through it."

Eyes like intricate marbles turned their greeny-blue light on me. "You got yourself through it."

"Well, I had a reason to." I lowered my bag to the floor by its strap, looked up. "You know we kind of had a deal?"

Her eyes went up to one side. "Hm, technically I'm not supposed to have favorites." She pushed her lips out, and they twisted the same way.

I smiled. "Well, I'm not a patient any more, am I?"

She slapped her thigh. "Oh, well, in that case..." She turned away. "I get off at seven."

A quick flick of her hair as she glanced over her shoulder with a chuckle. "Better get it over with."

Ten months later, holding hands, we emerged from a wood. Lumpy, springy turf leading outwards, inclining slightly, came to an end.

Kate gasped, because beyond lay the sea.

Seagulls cried below. Even up here, I could taste salt.

The sun closed with the offing, staining the lower sky's band of cloud pink. The sea still sparkled but in the form of an ever-changing road stretching from the sun almost to the shore.

Kate leaned against me. "It's breathtaking."

The light breeze caught me and I ran my hand through my full head of hair.

"Come on, I want to show you something." I pulled her with me towards the tussocky lip.

Her hand shot to her mouth when she peered down.

Both of us stared at the words scored in the sand:

Will you
marry me?

Flattened-out waves, little more than successive lines of foam, lapped the top of the beach.

I got down on one knee, produced a tiny box from my pocket and opened it to disclose the ring I'd bought. "Kate Crishaw, will you make me the happiest man on earth?"

She clapped a hand to her mouth. "Oh, Paul. Yes. Yes! Of course I will."

A smile gripped my face.

"I love you to death." Jumping up, I clasped her to me. "And back."

She wrapped her arms around me and lifted her lips to mine. I savored her mouth, warm, wet, familiar.

We came up for air just in time to catch the sinking sun wink once and disappear.

Rosy clouds still garlanded the sky, yet the day dimmed.

Together, we turned towards the wood. She was putting the ring on— "It fits perfectly"—when she suddenly raised her gaze.

"Oh, my God," she cried, stopping.

Colors paintballed the wood. This portion of it, above and around the pathway through it, blazed with red, orange, yellow, green and blue bulbs.

Piano music tinkled from concealed speakers.

Kate laughed. "Paul, you crazy, crazy man."

I smiled, spread out my hands. "Well, how often do you meet the love of your life?"

We kissed again, above the sunset's golden coronet and beneath the wood spattered with light.

I look up to see the Devil looking at me. "I was supposed to go first, not her. It was meant to be me." I'm poking myself in the chest with my thumb.

The Devil lowers his head. "I understand your anger. Losing her must be like having your heart ripped out of you still beating."

I put a hand to my chest, draw breath. "It is. Her kindness, her cheekiness, snuffed out. It just doesn't make sense, doesn't seem real." I sniff, exhale. "Love, to me, is a lot like getting religion." Different parts of my face tug in different directions. "Oh." I raise a hand. "No offence."

The Devil smiles. "You'll find we're a lot less touchy here."

"What I mean is, love changes everything. It reconfigures your mind, your whole world." My voice cracks. I gabble just to get everything out that I need to: "Our hearts were like two walkie talkies that always kept the channel open. I made jokes just to hear her laugh. I loved her bones, loved her blood. When she slept, I could see all the way back to the girl she once was. Someone you..." It feels like something folds in my throat. I grip the sides of my chair, cough to try and clear it. "...love, trust and desire. She was all those things to me and more. That's what I wanted to explain to Him."

The Devil turns his head to scratch behind his ear. "And

how was it when you turned up there? Did they give you a debriefing?"

"You could say that." I sigh.

Chapter 5

Gate-Crashing Heaven

"Right, pants down, bend over."

Having stooped to put my shoes back on, I reared up. I'd already had my fingerprints taken and been flashbulbed for a mugshot. I'd just stepped through a metal detector and been frisked, poked and prodded. I drew the line at the insertion of a digit.

We'd been ordered into two lines, men on one side, women on the other. Both queues stretched all the way down the long hall, with staff in white coats at this end and suited officials at desks at the other. The room had creaking floorboards and smelt of sawdust. Bare bulbs hung from the center of the ceiling at regular intervals. Dark-uniformed guards stood or patrolled in the shadows to either side with their arms folded around semi-automatic weapons.

Everyone else stood patiently waiting in line, shuffling forwards when required. Why did I have to be assessed? Couldn't those in charge see that I was gate-crashing heaven? Or maybe they could.

"Bend over," came the instruction again.

Only a waist-high partition around this section protected one's modesty.

I looked for Kate ahead. I couldn't see the back of her blonde head anywhere. Grey crowded out the other colors.

"Kate! Kate!" I called.

The man trying to search me spoke into the small walkie-talkie attached, upside down, to the lapel of his white coat. "Internal Examination, line 1. Got a live one."

Guards beelined from all angles.

"Hey—What's—" Two of them grabbed me by my underarms and dragged me off to the side. "I'm just—"

A door opened as if on a pulley and we flew down a corridor with my toecaps skittering this way and that across tiled flooring.

More boots followed as we turned one corner, another.

We stopped halfway along a corridor with metal doors all down one side.

"Right," said one of the guards, as the two holding me turned me around to face the others and relaxed their grip.

Did it really take six of them?

One opened the nearest door.

I peered at a small drab space that would have been grey if it wasn't for the graffiti that had crawled up and around and all over the walls.

"What?" I said.

The twitch of a semi-automatic. "In."

"Hey, what am I supposed to have done?" I cried.

Bristling guns won the argument. I stepped into the tiny cell.

After a couple of hours, they let me out.

Blinking, shaking. "What's wrong with this fucking place?"

How was I supposed to catch up with Kate now? Judging by the people we passed and the glimpses into cells and offices, there weren't any women in this part of the complex.

I glanced at my escort—two men in suits, one with slicked-back hair carrying an armful of folders and the other with a shaved head. They took me along a different combination of corridors to a room not much bigger than the cell but wide enough for a table.

"Sit," said the one with flattened hair, placing the folders on the table.

Framed by the blacked-out upper half of the wall behind them, they sat down opposite me. Between us rose a terminal and, next to it, what looked like recording equipment. One of them flicked a switch.

I smacked an armrest. "What is this place? Why are you keeping me here?"

The larger one with the shaved head shifted in his chair. It creaked under his bulk. "Everyone passes through here."

"Where's my wife?" I demanded. "I want to see my wife."

The one with dark, thinning, slicked-back hair fixed me with narrowing eyes. "The first thing you need to understand is that there can be no communication between the living and the dead."

"But—"

"None."

I threw up my hands. "Then what's the point of me *being* here?"

Though it was good to get confirmation I was still alive. That cell had had me questioning my own existence.

They didn't respond.

"Where did the others go?" I said.

The one with no hair flexed his fingers. "Your cohort, those approved, have been transferred to the periphery."

"Of heaven?"

"Yes."

"And the rest?"

He cracked his knuckles. "When you come here, normally there are two possible outcomes: onward admission into heaven; rejection and referral to hell."

The flat-haired one typed at the terminal.

"What is that thing?" I said.

"It's a soul reader," said the one with the shaved head. "We tell it things, it tells us things."

"Name?" said his colleague, without looking up.

"Paul Desuthe."

"Occupation?"

"I'm not sure that's relevant but... jingle writer."

More typing.

He tilted his head. "We don't have anything for that."

His eyes slid off to the side. They flicked back. "I'll put you down as Poet."

"Hah."

He ignored my half a laugh and carried on tapping. "Date of birth?"

"Listen," I said, "is all this really necessary?"

"We need to be sure all asylum seekers are genuine."

I prodded the tabletop. "I'm not planning to stay, I'm visiting."

He hit a key, glanced at his colleague. "Technically, anyone who hasn't been granted leave to remain is an illegal, with only a few exceptions."

The bald one leaned from one side to the other in his chair. "We need to check that you're not here to commit hostile acts."

"Hostile acts against what?"

"The system."

I rested an elbow on the table. "Why would I attack the system?"

"There are those who seek to undermine it."

I sat back, gripped the armrests. "Here?"

"Especially here."

"Who?"

"Undercover operatives, defectors..."

"Okay, this is doing my head in. Listen..." I sat up, held on to the edge of the table. "I don't need to see Kate now. I just want her back." I let go of the table, moved my hands apart. "So let me see God and I'll explain the situation to Him." I smiled. "A just deity will see the injustice."

The bald one pointed at the screen. The smaller one nodded.

I drummed my fingers on the edge of the desk. "Well?" I couldn't read their poker faces. "What's the verdict?"

Tap-tap-tap.

The one at the terminal looked up. "So your wife died, you think there's been a mistake and you're here to try and put things right?"

"Yes. That's what I've been telling you."

"Then, if on a technicality, we're duty bound to let you enter."

"What?" I glanced from one to the other. "Really?" I cocked my head. "What technicality?"

His gaze dropped to the terminal. "Compassionate grounds."

"Thank you." I stood up. "I'm not sure this whole rigmarole was necessary but, well..." I didn't push it.

"That's everything." His colleague turned off the recording equipment, pushed back from the terminal, and gathered the folders together. "While we're processing your papers, you're welcome to call or message ahead."

I opened my mouth.

"Him, not her."

I closed it again.

"When we're done, we'll assign you to a guide and see you to a transfer point."

Chapter 6

Interview with the Devil

"Know what they told me at the gate?" I ask the Devil as my chair squeaks beneath me. "That there were things I needed to know that would help make sense of it. Of the senseless!" Realizing I've raised my voice, I lower it. "I wasn't interested in *making sense* of anything. As soon as I got out of that place, I took off to confront Him."

Still with his feet up, the Devil crosses his ankles. "What were you going to do?"

I chew the inside of my cheek for a bit. "I don't know. Whatever it took."

His feet drop. "Well, what are your plans now?"

"I got ejected." I jerk my head upwards. "From there. And I need to get back."

The Devil stands, strides over to the window with his hands behind his back and peers out. I can see part of his reflection in the black window.

"You know, you created quite a stir bursting in there like that," he says without turning.

I scan the office in case there's anything I missed but, unlike his counterpart's, it's pretty bare. "Well, yes, it did seem to cause something of a security alert."

"I mean in both worlds." Leaning forwards, he touches the glass. "The two are closer than you think. Nothing happens in one without ramifications in the other."

I'm not sure what to say. I scratch the tip of my ear. "Injustice irks me, makes me want to do something about it."

His reflection's looking at me. I feel it even before I meet his gaze.

He swings round. "Would you say you have a problem with authority figures?"

I look one way, lean the other. "Well, I like to think for myself. But it's true, I have been rather... angry."

He slides his hands into his pockets. "Yes, so it would seem." He grins. "And any enemy of my... opposite number is a friend of mine."

I find myself smiling. "You seem..."

His head tilts. "Yes?"

I sit back. "Why do you let... the other side say all those terrible things about you?"

"Well, I have my reputation to think of." He laughs crossing the room. "You know, it's not easy to get back there, once you've been expelled. Some of us have been trying for a very long time." He stops an arm's length away.

Bracing my elbows against the arms of the chair, I sit up straight. "Oh. Well... I have to, somehow."

"Perhaps I might be able to tell you a way in return for a little bit of your... expertise." He extends a hand. "I help you, we help each other. What do you say?"

I look at the hand, look at him.

Kate's pale face flashes up on the screen of my mind in black and white.

I grasp his hand, shake it.

Chapter 7

On the Devil's Payroll

I'm working for the other side now. Of the Devil's party, you might say. Though the way I see it, at least the Devil's honestly bad. I'm not even convinced he's bad. He certainly hasn't been to me. I'm part of his media team. We write slogans in his defense trying to set the record straight, or at least muddy the waters a bit. I work in a building with what I often imagine to be an infinite number of rooms. It's filled with not just copywriters but artists and musicians and film-makers and programmers. It's a bit like going back to college. Here I have freedom to think. No one tells me what to do. I don't even have fixed hours. At any time, I can go where and do whatever I like. Though I'd rather keep busy. It takes my mind off things. Not that I've forgotten my ultimate goal. Far from it.

When I'm at work, I often take a coffee and my laptop out to one of the communal areas. At the moment I'm in a café two floors above my floor. Its glass walls offer a line of sight to the bridge that connects this building to the next, where the Devil spends much of his time.

The espresso machine grunts and gurgles and I inhale the heady aroma of coffee beans. I'm on my second cup when I spot my employer crossing the bridge. His retinue accompanies him, dressed mostly in black. He enters and nods when he sees me but, with all of them around, it's impossible to get a chance to talk to him, so I remain seated.

A short man in glasses says something, and the Devil slaps him on the back. "What do you think this is, Ray, a holiday camp?"

The short man looks up and around.

"Don't answer that," says the Devil, laughing.

Several of the new arrivals peek in my direction and I spot a couple of elbow nudges.

Hushed voices cancel each other out but I overhear a woman say something about "a big push".

A man with a gap between two very white front teeth glances at me before glaring at a pale, painfully thin woman with red hair.

"Ssh!" he hisses.

Gem, the Devil's assistant, is with them. She gives me a wave, detaches herself from the group and comes over.

The rest of the newcomers find seats around the Devil until all I can see is the top of his head.

Gem's wearing black lipstick, a black dress, ripped nets and ankle-length boots with laces all the way up. Her necklace is an upside-down crucifix.

She smiles. "Hey, Paul."

I smile back. "Hi."

She sets herself down and now that she's off the stilts of her shoes, taking up so little of the chair, I can see through her gothy makeup to the girl underneath. Younger than I remember, perhaps just teens, she shouldn't be in one of the destinations of the dead.

How did she wind up here?

Her sleeveless dress showcases the tattoos garlanding her arms. What is that? Roses wrapped with meat?

I make out bones, muscle, veins. Representing dissections to various depths, the tattoos depict the inner workings of her arms.

Just her arms?

"How are you?" she says.

I wipe my hand across my mouth. "Not bad. You?"

"Good, thanks."

I stick my finger in a bit of wet coffee on the table-top and smear it round in a circle. "Mind if I ask you something?"

Her hair swings from side to side.

I stop playing with the spillage to point beyond the closed glass bridge. "What's that other building all about?"

She touches a finger to her lips, lowers her voice. "It takes your kind of work to the next level."

I half chuckle, half cough. "I'm not even sure what that means."

She tilts her head, smiles. "It's shrouded in secrecy at the moment but everyone will know eventually. Here, there. Back home."

I stare at her. "I thought everything here was access-all-areas."

Her hair falls back in front of her face as she leans forwards. "Well, most of it is. We just have to guard against infiltrators, spies, that sort of thing."

I glance around at the others. "There can't be that many, can there?"

"You'd be surprised." She lifts her hair out of her face. "So what's it like there? You're the only person I know who's been." She's looking around now. "Most people either come here or go there."

"Not as you'd expect. Pretty much like here, only the other way around."

Her head lists. "What's that mean?"

"The place is overrun with rules and restrictions."

"Ah, yeah, here the only rule is no rules." She shakes with laughter but the laughter stops and the shaking carries on in the form of a shudder. Her face contorts. "We hate it there."

"What is it that gets you about it?" Taking a sip of coffee, I peer over the top.

She blows a strand of hair out of her face and pauses to scratch above her eyebrow. Just below where the cadaverous tattoos start, I spot a scar across her wrist.

Her other arm rests on the table on its side and an identical scar runs across that wrist.

Now she's fiddling with her necklace. "Personally?"

Maintaining eye contact so she doesn't know I've seen, I nod.

My cup rattles against its saucer as I replace it.

"Oh, I think the exclusivity of it," she says.

She leans her head to one side, stares at me out of one eye. "You were lucky to even get there."

"Well, I didn't last long." I crack a smile.

She frowns. "That's not what the Devil says."

"Oh?"

She glances round as her boss pushes up from his table and half the room gets to its feet. She jumps up. "Talk soon. Better get back."

I open my mouth but she's gone before I can ask her what she means.

I don't let things go. After yesterday, I take my laptop to the bridge between the two halves of the building and sit on one of the lounge chairs halfway along it. There's a small table between me and the next chair and a potted plant the far side of that.

More floors up than I care to think about, the city twinkles in front of me and, in reflection, behind.

One end of the bridge is completely open, with access to the café and the whole of my building. The other is barred by a steel security door with a small square window at eye level.

I looked through earlier but couldn't see anything. Just doors.

Today I'm in luck. The steel door opens and the Devil comes striding along the mid-air glass corridor. The door clunks behind him. He's on his own.

He's got a couple of files under his arm, which he lowers with his other hand. "Hi, Paul. How's it going?"

"Good, thank you." I raise an arm. "Can I just ask...?" He stops. "What's that side all about?" I'm pointing to the building he's just left.

"Well, if you're the software in the anti-propaganda machine, that's the hardware."

I clear my throat, look up. "What kind of hardware?"

He waves a hand as if wafting away a fly. "Oh, plenty of time for that." He chuckles as he faces me. "Fancied a change of outlook, did you?"

He pivots and continues on his way.

"Er..." I never quite know how to address him. "No, it's just... I can't afford to get too comfortable."

He pauses, turns. "Oh? Why's that?"

I lower my head and rub my eye. "You haven't forgotten our..." I look up. He's blurred but quickly comes back into focus. "..arrangement, have you? Only, I'll have to be moving on soon."

"Paul, Paul, Paul..." He stops in front of me. "You wouldn't believe the amount of preparation going on behind the scenes to get you where you need to be." I wouldn't? He smiles. "So, trust me, all's in hand, my friend. All's in hand." Making time like a down-to-earth billionaire, he crouches at my side. "Going well?" He peers at the laptop's screen. "'Deliver us from goodness.'" He laughs. "Like it. And 'The Devil loves you.'" He clicks his fingers. "Snappy." He stands, claps me on the shoulder. "You know what? Some of my counsel had doubts about you simply because you'd set foot in the other place. A few even suspected you of being sent to spy." He pauses. I take a breath. "But don't worry, I told them where your loyalties lie." He grips my shoulder. "There's a vacancy and I've been wondering who I could find to fill it." He lets go. "How would you like to be my PR manager? Effective immediately."

I look up. His counsel? Doubts? I've barely time for these pinpricks of thought. My mouth opens, shuts, opens again. "Your—Really?"

He smiles. "I think you're ready for the responsibility. Why not?"

"Thank you... Thank you very much." I clasp his hand, shake it.

From lowly copywriter to the Devil's PR man? My meteoric descent continues apace.

Chapter 8

The Devil's Peep Show

"Ladies and gentlemen, for your savage amusement to-night..."

Now that I've been promoted, I spend a lot more time with the great man himself. Hell has its own TV channel and the Devil has his own show, filmed before a live—or should that be dead?—audience. I stand next to him in the wings as a woman in glasses with her hair in a chignon bun, in a slim-fit black suit and heels, introduces him.

She exits the far side, and the Devil strides onstage in trousers and shirtsleeves, rolled up, to receive his applause.

He wheels to face the cameras. "People ask me, about earth, 'God's got all those imposing buildings, everyone devoted to him. What have you got?'" A pause. "The Devil's got everything else, I tell them. The Devil has everything else."

Laughter from the ranks of seats.

The crinkliness of a smile, side on.

The lines disappear just as quickly. "In the war between good and evil, you can't be neutral. You have to pick a side." He raises his arms as if to embrace his audience. "And I hope we all know which side we're on?"

A cheer from the hall.

One arm drops.

As if reaching for the studio lights, he sticks a hand out into the auditorium right in front of a camera. "Earth is a battlefield between heaven and hell and, soon, friends, it'll be our move." He closes that hand.

With his other, he produces some kind of controller from his pocket and turns to the area behind him. "Let's take a look, shall we?"

A spinning earth fills the space.

The controller dips as he presses it.

Earth stops dead. Expanding to fill our field of vision and carrying on expanding, the globe gives way to a continent, gives way to a country, gives way to clouds, gives way to ground, which tips on its side as we're about to smash into it. Now we're stationary and everything else is moving.

No, we're coasting laterally... in a vehicle.

We rotate slowly on an axis at or near the center of a stretched-out car. A man in a Ralph Lauren suit comes into view seated in the rear. He gets out his iPhone and we catch a glimpse of his TAG Heuer watch before he passes out of shot. A city street slides by from right to left. The towers that border it have more in common with the sky than they do with the earth. Way up front, the back of a driver's head rotates around us. Now streets slide by from left to right, until we return to the man in the suit.

We stay on him.

He's got a hand over the phone to his ear and a finger in the other ear.

"Hi, Steve. What are they asking?" His head jerks. "What?" A pause. "Well, buy, buy, buy." His head shakes with the force with which he utters the word. "What? No, I don't care if it's 1.4 million. It's only gonna go *up*. Buy, goddam it, buy."

I jump when I see the Devil again, with the globe behind him. It's as if someone's ripped a VR headset off me.

"Right," he says. I've got my hand to my chest because my heart's jumping around inside it. "Let's flick to the other side of the world, shall we?"

The globe spins, stops, and we plummet back in.

Shearing off before hitting the ground, we slow to cruise dust-caked streets at head height.

Intact but pockmarked buildings give way to geometrical ruins with upper floors and walls jutting out over nothing.

Bars stick out of concrete at odd angles; reinforced steel, bent.

We turn left, right, and each street is the same: shells of apartments next door to rubble.

Glancing behind as if right at us, a girl of five or six runs three or four meters ahead of us.

We catch up with her and bob to avoid jutting pipes, dangling cables, screes of debris.

After dropping under a web of wires, we remain roughly at her height.

I can hear her shaky, all-over-the-place breathing and the frantic slap-slap-slap of her tiny flip-flops.

The clap of a shot and she leaps. She lands and one of her flip-flops turns the wrong way, comes off.

We stop next to it.

She runs on, away from us, over the stony street.

Turning somewhere up and behind us, a jet whines.

The girl looks round.

The jet screams.

The whites of her eyes get bigger as she presses her hands to her ears.

A flash obliterates her and the buildings. I'm about to duck before a swelling cloud of debris engulfs us but the eruption of sound's cut short.

Girl and city have gone.

Gasps and howls from the audience.

The Devil's holding a hand up on the stage. I'm plunging for breath.

Bent over, clutching my chest, I peer up. His hand's now a fist. "And they call *this* hell." I straighten up. He's lowering and shaking his head. He raises it. "So there you have it. Two snapshots of earth. Ruled by you-know-who." He looks around his audience. "Which is why what is needed is a change at the top."

I'm in the middle of turning away.

My head snaps back. Change? At the top? Did I hear right? My insides fizz at such dark, seditious suggestions. Yet amid all the applause, the cheering, it's as if I'm being reconstituted. The fizzing dies down, eases completely, because I know he's right. Extreme as it is, that's the solution.

How could humanity have got the Devil so wrong?

Chapter 9

The Plot Against God

I'm sat in my office (I have my own now that I've been pro-moted) drafting a speech for the Devil for his next TV show.

Actually, I'm staring out of the window at casinos and hotels and nightclubs and bars and restaurants. What would Kate make of it here? She'd probably have loved it. Instead, she's stuck in joyless heaven.

The door opens and I quickly look down, round, up.

My employer's put his head through the gap. "Still want your revenge on the person responsible for your wife's death?" A tilt of the head. "I don't mean the other driver."

I'm nodding. "I still need to have it out with Him, yes."

The Devil's head jerks up and off to the side as he turns away.

I get up and follow him out.

Finally. It's happening.

The Devil meant everything he said.

He's wearing a dark suit. I'm in jeans and a short-sleeved shirt. We stride up corridors, climb a few floors, more corridors, and turn corners until I don't know which way we're facing or whereabouts in the building we are.

When we come out by the glass wall of the café, through a door I've never noticed before, I halt.

It's as if my mind's held up and arrives a little later.

The Devil hasn't stopped. He carries straight on across the bridge.

I catch up with him at the door to the other building.

He punches in a number on a keypad, a buzzer sounds and the steel door clicks open.

We pass through and up a corridor with doors either side, turning up another corridor with just one door, at the end, which leads down a tiled stairwell with stainless steel railings. The lighting's low, tinged red. We keep going, down and round, round and down.

"Why are you helping me?" I say.

"You're going to help me."

My mouth's dry. My tongue feels thick inside it. "How?"

"That's what you're about to find out."

We continue our clattering descent.

Eventually we emerge into what must be hell's lowest basement. With its high concrete walls, it's like a giant nuclear bunker. We're at the top. Staggered metal gantries stretching all the way around give an unimpeded view of a central dais at the bottom, half illuminated, half not.

Our footsteps clang on gridded treads, down one of the diagonal aisles, past men and women in black uniforms standing or seated at screens and consoles.

Level with the Devil now, I glance at him. "Why me?"

"You're an unbound."

My head swings back. "A what?"

"An unbound. It's what we call people who are still living their lives and have freedom to roam. Most don't. They're assigned to a destination, and that's it." He pats me on the shoulder. "Because of your special status, you have greater leeway. That makes you important in ways you don't yet realize." A colleague raises the flat of his right hand to the peak of his cap, stiffly. The Devil returns the salute. "That and other things."

"What..." My head's wagging between them. "What other things?"

The Devil takes off his jacket. "You think for yourself, which makes you dangerous. In uncertain times, a potential key player for either side." He swings his jacket over his shoulder. "You could say that it upsets the balance between heaven and hell."

Now that we're almost there, I can see the podium's a vast model.

We hit the bottom.

Standing at waist height, the model's divided into two halves by a partition. The nearest half is bathed in light. The far half is in darkness but with miniature buildings lit up from within and tiny streetlights aglow. Both halves have numbers and symbols projected onto them. Many of these are moving.

I stare at the cruciform tower with the security gate around it and the airport this side and the constellation of lights burning holes in the darkness beyond and I know what this is. It's a replica of heaven next to a replica of hell.

"How come they're side by side?" I ask.

The Devil chuckles without smiling. "The idea of one above the other is charmingly archaic."

"But the darkness here that covers everything, it..." I put my hand up to my temple. "And the lift... it fell."

"Some illusions are preserved but that is what they are, illusions." He studies the restless symbols and numbers. "Heaven and hell occupy the same space, or different parts of it. The one only exists at the other's expense." His hand turns over. "The lift is just a crude representation of the disjunction between the two."

He twists in my direction. "You've heard of the military build-up over there?"

I scratch a scab on my elbow. From the accident? "Heard it? I've seen it."

He nods with his head to one side. "Yes, of course. Well, that's what we're responding to, and time, well..." His forehead crinkles. "There isn't any." He compresses his lips, raises his eyebrows, forges on. "They're all for putting up walls. I'm all for tearing them down. It's a lot to take in, I know. Contrary to everything you've been taught, the prisoners of heaven need freeing." Resting one hand on the edge of the model, he leans against it. "What I'm proposing is the liberation of the enslaved, both in heaven and on earth, and…" His hand sweeps over the board. "..the reunification of heaven and hell." He fixes me with his gaze. "You've been helping to change minds but the truth is, we're never going to win like that." He stands upright. "Unfortunately, the only way to fight military might is with military might." One hand makes a chopping motion. "It's time to topple the tyrant."

I take a long breath. "And where do I come into all this?"

He points at heaven's section. "You're going in through the back door to let us in through the front."

The Devil's staff, generals, whatever they are, step down from their posts to join him around the model. Despite their civilian clothes then and uniforms and peaked caps now, I recognize some of their faces from that day in the café.

"The I-sixes are doing their last checks," says the pale, bony woman.

"The Star-beams are ready to roll," says the man with the gap in his teeth.

I don't understand any of it. All I know is my small part in the plan is to go in first, accost God and let the Devil in.

As his advisors confer and plot strategies, the Devil escorts me back up towards the door. Our footsteps clang in unison. His hand settles on my shoulder. "You'll go far, Paul." Clap-clap. "I've high hopes for you." His hand alights again, grips. "Even the Devil has disciples, you know."

With a start, I glance round.

His arm drops.

He's looking down, through the tiny lozenge-shaped holes in the steps. "Tomorrow's the day we reclaim what's rightfully ours." We stop at the door and he looks up, smiles. "And of course, when I'm in charge of both regions and the border's demolished, I can relax the rules. You and your wife could be reunited." My heart vaults. I could visit Kate in heaven. I'm so busy picturing her and I running towards each other, across the border, that I don't notice what it is the Devil's passing me until it's in my hands. "We'll aim for minimum casualties. But of course, they'll have to be one."

I stare down at the glinting implement, hold it in one hand.

"You know what to do," I hear.

I pocket the knife in a trance. My heart thuds. A pulse flutters in my neck. I can't speak.

I nod, with my heart in my mouth.

Chapter 10

War on Heaven

A black army rolls across the desert. The combined blaze of its headlights illuminates a gigantic gate set inside a wall that stretches as far as I can see upwards and to either side.

This is the first time I've seen the border close up. I've no idea what it's made of. Stone? Metal? Some other kind of material altogether? It's dark but smooth and if it wasn't for the faint outline of the gate, and the fact I know there's a whole world on the other side, I'd have assumed it was solid and that was that.

I'm sitting in the back of a jeep with my arm hooked over the side. The Devil's standing next to me, leaning against the roll bar. We're parked at an angle on a dune.

He's wearing an officer's uniform, complete with peaked cap. I'm in my civvies.

Row by row, black tanks lurch to a halt around us.

Giant troop carriers, with wheels as big as car-crushing monster trucks', draw up in the background.

Gunship helicopters whip up whirlwinds of sand as they come to rest at intervals, in front, in between, behind.

The thwacking of multiple sets of rotor blades winds down to the dying whine of the engines.

The growly, grumbling tanks fall quiet one by one.

A black-helmeted soldier sticking up out of the turret of the nearest tank dips his head. He holds a microphone closer to his lips to speak, then raises his gaze to the wall.

The gate remains shut.

The Devil reaches forwards, taps the jeep's driver on the shoulder. "Right, Petra, let's go."

Gears crunch, engage, and we roll, slipping, slow-motion sliding down the slope. I hang on as the vehicle swings around and we thread back through the tanks.

The Devil sits down, turns to me. "Everything hinges on you now, Paul."

I chew my cheek. I haven't slept. My heart's jackhammering and every muscle in my body's taut.

I could leap out of the jeep.

We pass mobile rocket launchers going the other way on one side, armored vehicles towing heavy artillery on the other.

I lean away from the Devil to stare at him. "You said there'd be minimal casualties."

"Well, yes, but they're hardly going to capitulate if they think they can beat us, are they?" He tips his head to one of his generals, who salutes from the rear seat of another jeep, before turning back to me. "And you of all people know how prepared they are." He touches his knuckles to my shoulder. "Besides, if you do what you're supposed to, there'll be no loss of life."

I stiffen. "Well, one."

The Devil's smile shrinks and fades. "Yes, one life or the lives of billions." He lowers his arm. "But I'm gambling everything on you making the right decision." He prods his knee to the beat of his speech. "Because if you want to be reunited with your wife, this is what you need to do."

Sticking out through the hole it's made in my pocket, inside my trousers, the cold blade presses against my leg, flat side on.

The fluttering starts up in my neck.

My stomach churns.

I ride out the bumps from the neck down and try and shut out my surroundings so I can think. If I do what the Devil demands, would I even have Kate's love at the end of it? What would she make of it all? The only vaguely similar dilemma I ever discussed with her was to do with contracts and friendship.

I remember sitting down with her in the kitchen with my elbows on the table and my head in my hands. "I've got this situation, at work. I can't talk about it. NDAs and all that." I looked up. "But what would you do if you had to choose between what's right and what's necessary?"

With her face smooth and serious, she stares at me. "You have to do what's right, every time."

Already, just across from me at our pine table, she's fading.

I nod, heavily.

"But what your own heart tells you is right," I hear, "or necessary," a postscript I don't recollect, as if she's communicating with me here, now, opening up the way for hope and reunion on one side, allowing my heart to expand, and—it clenches—murder on the other.

Losing my balance, I rock in my seat and my shoes scuff against the hollow-sounding floor before I get a purchase and straighten up.

The Devil's pushed me.

I look up, around.

We've stopped at the casino through which I entered his domain.

Then I notice he's got out.

Sluggishly, with utmost deliberateness to compensate for my limbs' reluctance to cooperate, I likewise get down.

What is this com-lag between brain and body? Tiredness?

We climb the steps, pass through a doorway, a lobby, and cross the bing-bonging entertainment hall. Still drugged with sleep, or lack of it, I lag behind. What are we even doing here? I ignore the people on stools, the heads turning, and follow the Devil to the other side.

I spot Gem at her old post.

She sees me and smiles.

"Give them hell," she says, laughing.

Empty head ringing, I force out a smile like the last bit of toothpaste from a flattened tube.

I follow her eyes, glance at the Devil. His gaze converges with hers where minus numbers rise above the pair of metal doors.

The lift's coming down, or over.

Head pulsing, I swing round to the Devil. "This is the way back...?" I mis-swallow and my throat closes up, which sets me hacking. "You mean I could have gone back at any time?" I get out, in between barks.

"No. This is strictly for heaven's rejects." He checks a nearby terminal on a stand. "Nobody goes the other way."

"Uh?" I'm utterly lost.

"Which is why they won't be expecting you. Your status hasn't been revoked." He cracks his knuckles. "You shouldn't trigger any security alerts."

I nod as if every word makes perfect sense.

The Devil leans close. "Don't sacrifice your wife. Would He save her? Did He?" God's rival lowers his voice. "No. It's just one little life." His jaw hardens. "A life for a life."

My head jerks with such suddenness, it's as if my mind crashes into the front of my skull. "But Kate's..." Not alive exactly. "...in heaven."

The Devil inhales as if inflating himself full of air, which comes out all in a rush: "In heaven's prison separated from you for good with no possibility of parole."

The sounds of the casino fade away as if a helmet's just been rammed down over my head. I can hear my own breathing, see Kate's pale face above me and feel the plip, plip, plip of her blood on my forehead as my heart booms in my ears.

Ping.

The door slides open.

"Russell, welcome!" Gem holds out a hand to the blinking, swaying arrival, who takes it as he exits.

The Devil offers me something. "Anyone gets in your way, use this." I take it before I've fully worked out what it is—a gun with a dart sticking out of the end of it. He also passes over a holster with loops all the way around it. Each loop contains a dart with a clear plastic cap over the end. "Don't worry, I know your scruples. They're tranquilizers. You'll simply be giving the person on the receiving end a very pleasant siesta."

His hand's on my shoulder as we head towards the lift. "Remember who ripped her away from you." A squeeze. "Remember who won't let you have her back." His hand lifts. "This way you can."

The outline of the knife digs into my leg with each step. Can I really do this?

And lose Kate again? How can I not?

I've no sooner crossed the threshold than the door seals itself shut behind me and I rise as if ascending to heaven with a mind chockfull of hell.

Chapter 11

God's Blind Spot

Ping.

I step out of the lift on the top floor, hasten around the corner and spot God's officious assistant.

Rocking on the carpet's stiff fibers, I move towards him.

He sees me, reaches under his desk, stands, and comes out from behind it. He's got his hand up.

I raise mine, with the tranquilizer gun in it.

"Don't get up on my account," I say, squeezing the trigger.

He goes down with a thud.

I pull out another dart, flip off the cap and attach it to the end of the gun.

Now that I'm closer to the desk, I can hear a faint but insistent bleep.

Remembering it from last time, I whirl around to see two Guardians in black. How did they get here so quickly?

"There's a word for those who switch sides," says the one on the left.

"Yeah. Fuckheads," says the other.

The Guardians look the same with their dark visors down but I'd recognize the voices of these two anywhere.

"Well, why the hell send me there, then?" I raise the tip of the dart gun and their helmets dip, fractionally, in time. "Don't worry, it won't hurt."

"This will," says the gruff one, extending his telescopic baton with a deft flick and a *chung-chung-chung.*

He raises it.

Soldierly clicks from his baton as he feints left, right.

His body armor doesn't leave much to aim at.

I fire. He scrabbles for his neck.

He's withdrawing the dart when he topples backwards.

I reload.

"Don't..." His colleague's on my right.

"...do this..." Then he's on my left.

"...Paul." He's standing in front of me, too close for me to use the gun. It's lowered between us.

I pull the trigger.

I almost bump my head on his helmet as we both look down.

The dart's sticking out of his boot.

He lifts his foot. "There's..."

"Yes?"

Wobbling, he places his foot back on the floor. "You don't under..."

He sways.

"What?" I reach down, pull out the dart for him, straighten up. "Tell me."

He crumples.

Sighing, I turn and holster the gun.

I pull my microphone closer to my mouth. "Clear."

"Right, get in there," says the Devil.

My earpiece whistles as I hurry through the doorway.

"In."

"There's something I need you to do first."

"Yes?" I stoop for no—outward—reason and glance upwards, at the door I'd originally taken for a cupboard before, ready to do anything except what I'm supposed to be doing, turning and raising my head.

"See the contraption on the desk?"

"Yes."

The mechanical monstrosity beyond the terminal is still clacking, clanking, and whirring as if the universe depends upon it.

"Okay, good, now, press the red lever."

I go over.

I can see other levers, a yellow lever and a blue, but not a red. Then I spot it, round the side, next to a pendulum and a mesh of gears. "Okay, pressing now."

Nothing's happened.

I'm looking down when the faintest of shudders runs through the building.

As if to prove I didn't imagine it, it happens again.

An alarm blares and a voice, not in my earpiece this time, says, "Repair to the bunkers. This is not—repeat, *not*—a drill. Repair to the bunkers."

"What's going on?"

No answer.

I dash over to the window, peer out.

"Repair to the bunkers," resumes the voice.

A door's opened on the horizon. Tiny black vehicles surge into the light. Buildings ahead of them flash and balls of smoke erupt that lift into the air like so many hot-air balloons.

Black jets streak through the gap. They turn and head for the airport, where silver jets trundle up taxiways.

The sleek darts of the Devil's planes line up with the runway. Instead of coming in to land, they fly over it. Bombs drop and explode all the way down it.

The black planes climb, bank and, fanning out, come back in perpendicular to the airport. Missiles detach from their wings, accelerate ahead and dip to pierce the scattering jets, which burst into flames.

Above the black army swarming in, the first of many helicopters zips through the portal.

The floor tremors are constant now and accompanied by rattling from the desk and shelves as explosions go off closer and closer to the tower. Some of the jets have turned their firepower on the city. I can see flames pouring up-wards out of the sides of buildings that were intact just seconds ago.

Like a hard-boiled fly, the lead helicopter rises and falls, drifts to left and right.

For all its ducking and diving, I know it's headed this way.

"How come they've started?" I say into the mouthpiece.

"It's up to you to stop it. You can stop it all," intones the Devil. "You know what to do."

I glance in the distance at the segment of the city in flames. My heart's galloping because that's the suburbs of heaven, where the dead live.

Kate, I won't let you die twice.

My stomach gurgles and glug-glug-glugs.

I've opened the gates of hell. I can't sink any lower. Can I?

Grasping the hilt of the dagger in my pocket and withdrawing it, I step over to the inner door and turn the handle.

Chapter 12

The Assassination of God

I'm inside a white cube with a gleaming floor crossing towards what can only be the sanctum of sanctums.

Pleated curtains hang from a rectangular track suspended from the ceiling.

I stop a few feet away from where the two halves overlap, enough not to be able to see in, and stare at the dagger. Is this all it takes?

Procrastinating even now, right to the end, I run the blade across the pad of my finger and don't feel anything at all. Yet when I take it away, there's a red line rapidly filling with blood.

I daren't move or open my mouth to breathe in case the pummeling of my heart gives me away. I place a hand to my chest to try and contain it. Somehow, I've got caught up in the war between heaven and hell and I can't see a way out.

The building shakes.

Through my earpiece: "Better hurry up. They're dying down there. More and more of them all the time." He must be aware I can't reply. Not now, in here, so close. "You know me. I don't want anyone to die who doesn't need to, and especially not your wife." A crackle. "...only one who does."

With every delay the death count ticks upwards but I can stop it with one last addition to the tally.

Holding the dagger out in front of me, I approach the point where the two halves of curtain meet. My bowels bubble as if boiling. What happened? What did I do?

When did my fate become locked in? How far back? I paid the Devil a social visit and somehow my soul got lost on the baggage carousel. Did I really have any choice at all?

In a sense, it's already happened. I'm God's killer.

Yanking back the curtain, I make the lunge.

Chapter 13

The Devil's Coup d'État

My chest feels empty, crushed. I strain to draw breath.

I watch a smoking tower crumple, concertina in upon itself, sending out a billowing wave of dust in every direction and leaving a column of smoke where it had stood.

The smoke slowly drifts, to reveal nothing.

I'm standing in the office, staring out at all the blackened and burning buildings and the gaps where buildings that have already fallen used to be—the destruction, the desecration, of heaven—when the window darkens.

Facing inwards, one of hell's helicopters rises, sinks a little, bobs gently level with me. Rotor blades blur. The multi-paned window shuts out the sound.

Both helmeted occupants of the chopper have their visors down but these curve over and away from their noses and, apart from bendy microphones, leave the lower halves of their faces free.

I recognize the Devil's grin.

He waves from the co-pilot's seat, stops.

"Is it done?" He lip-syncs to his own voice.

I lower my head. "Yes."

"Right, see the intercom?"

I slouch over to the desk. "Yes."

"Unclick the green button and click the red one."

The Devil continues to observe from the compound eye of his wraparound visor in the floating bubble of the chopper's cockpit.

Standing side on, I push the one button lightly to release it, push the other right in so that it stays down.

A blue light goes off and a red one comes on.

Turning to the pilot, the Devil jabs a gloved finger in the direction of the rotor blades. The pilot nods and the aircraft tilts back, rises.

In my ear: "Get a move on. I need the hatch open."

Hidden speakers whistle, whine, as I leave the office and, like switching from mono to surround sound, now I can hear the same voice all around me, from different rooms, different floors: "Attention. This is your new God speaking." The helicopter's skids thunk down on the roof. "Your old God is no more." A hiss of static. "...very differently from now on. There's been a change of management."

I bite a chunk of the inside of my cheek.

I can't believe I let the Devil in.

Chapter 14

Resistance

Lifting the lid of the hatchway, I climb the last few steps and emerge onto the deck into the superabounding blue and a vortex trying to push me backwards, sideways, off the roof. Rotor blades smack-smack-smack the air.

Facing this way, the black helicopter's firmly planted on a white H inside a yellow circle inside a white square.

In the cramped cockpit, as the rotor blades unblur above him, the Devil pulls off his helmet, undoes his straps.

I watch him climb out.

With back bent, he runs in a long curve over to me in my corner.

Standing at right angles to each other, facing inwards, doesn't leave much room, and it feels as if my right leg's longer than my left. I've got one foot on the lid of the hatch.

An explosion hundreds of feet below rocks the building and the two of us sway, in time, both of us dangerously close to our respective edges.

Beneath the winding down of the helicopter, the pop-pop-pop of gunfire.

I turn to the Devil. "You said it would stop if..."

He waves a hand out over the edge. "There's pockets of resistance. If they won't lay down their weapons, what can we do?" Spotting me still staring at him, he throws an arm up and out. "Heaven's not the namby-pamby paradise everyone imagines. It's a military stronghold!"

"To protect against you!" It tears out of me.

"Oh, for hell's sake!" He stalks away up the edge, spins round. "You can't go back on this now."

"You think?" I run towards him, push, hard.

His arm goes up in a gesture he doesn't have time to complete. Stepping backwards at an angle, he plummets out of sight.

Chapter 15

Rooftop Revelations

Inhaling shakily in the shock of the moment, I tip my head back.

Lowering, righting, it, I let out the longest of exhalations.

I've done it. I've beaten the Devil.

The sound of the pilot firing up the helicopter again blasts me out of my reverie.

I spin round and his mouth's opening and closing in the goldfish bowl of the cockpit as he hits switches in front of him, above him. He grabs the controls and the chopper jerks, tilts, turns on the end of one candy-cane shaped skid and slews off the edge of the building to twirl, corkscrew, downwards.

I lean out after it.

Only a third of the way down but still far enough for a body to crush itself, the Devil lies on one of the outstretched arms of the tower.

As if at the end of a very long rope, the helicopter jerks to a halt level with him.

The pilot would have more than enough room to land on the projection if he wanted to, yet hangs back.

I'm so busy wondering why he isn't attempting to retrieve his master's body that it's a moment before I notice the Devil.

He's rubbing his head.

That's im...

He's sitting up.

But...

He gets up.

No...

He leans his head from side to side as if uncricking his neck.

Shielding his eyes, he looks up.

The laugh in my ear makes me jump. "You really think it'd be that easy? I've survived greater falls than that."

He strides towards the angle between the projection and the tower, places one foot on the vertical, then the other.

No no no no no...

He's walking up the side of the building.

Maybe hell is below us after all.

In my ear: "You've offended both sides now. So where do you think you're going to go?"

I step away from the edge, scan the cleft horizon. My heart's trying to thump its way out of me. My breathing's all over the place. "Back to earth... where I should have stayed."

"Oh? You think it's that simple?"

I press my finger to the earpiece. "What?"

"You can't."

I sidle back over to the edge, peer down. "Why not?"

The Devil stamps on a window, which holds. "Well, how are you going to get there for one thing?"

I haven't considered this till now.

I sway a little on the edge. "I... I don't know."

"You were held at the detention center before they gave you leave to remain, yes?"

"Yes."

"So how did you get there?"

"Well, I... I mean, I just..." I remember sobbing and pleading in the crushed car. "I prayed."

"And what's your last memory of your wife?"

I merely have to describe what I can see because, as clearly as with the Devil's eye-in-the-sky, it's as if I'm back there or, dangerous so close to the edge, as if she's right in front of me. "She's hanging in her seatbelt with blood pouring from the wound to her head."

"And then you came here?"

"Determined to see God, yes." I take an abortive breath and my sinuses deploy like miniature air-bags in my face. "Even when I knew I couldn't see her."

"What would you say if I told you she's still alive?"

The helicopter buzzsaws around and around the tower, a little higher each time.

I rub my eye. "I know she is, in a way."

"Not in heaven." A *chock* from his tongue. "That living death... No, I mean *alive* alive. On earth."

My mind stalls. "You... But... All the blood..."

"Head wounds. They bleed the most. Didn't you know? Type in her name at any terminal to see if you don't believe me, or simply want to watch her have sex with the next guy." My heart double claps. Kate's alive. She's okay. I try and ignore the last bit. What am I doing here? I need to find the way out, down whatever fire escape or laundry chute will lead me back. "It isn't your wife that died." I'm almost not listening, because there's no reason for me to be here now. "It's you."

A slap from my heart.

I'm listening now. "What?"

"You can't remember because death is the dream from which no one wakes up." His voice drops: "Punctured lung, if you want to know." I clutch my thorax as the reality crashes over me as hard, and soft, as a wave. He continues at normal volume: "When they said make sense of things, they meant your death, not your wife's. They didn't let you go because you were still alive. An unbound is someone in denial about being dead." I put my hands up to my head, dig my fingers into my temples, turn, stagger on the edge. "They're given greater freedom and their files are left open a bit longer because in many ways they're still living their lives. You're supposed to leave them be, let them blunder around like sleepwalkers until they bump into something and realize it for themselves." The Devil raises both arms and stretches. "So how does it feel to finally wake up? Or rather..." A snort. "...not."

I peer down, dredge my voice up from the depths of my being: "You sick bastard."

The Devil chucks his head back and laughs in my ears. "Well, I guess that's progress of sorts."

I clench and unclench my hands. "You're not going to get away with this."

"Ah, that, my friend, is where you're wrong. Thanks to you, I already have. And if you think you're somehow going to get out of it, you signed." His voice turns clicky and although I can't quite make it out yet, I know he's smiling. "The 'visitor's book', remember? Nice touch, that, I always think." Click-click. "There are no 'visitors' in hell. You're already mine."

I lower my chin against my chest. "Tricked from the start."

"Well, maybe a nudge here, a helping hand there. But you arrived almost like a gift from my illustrious neighbor as was. Something was needed to break the deadlock between heaven and hell and you were it. With your grief, your monomania, you were perfect for our purposes. An unbound with a poet's... innocence." A guffaw.

Looking around, I spot and reach for a pair of chocks. Dangling them over the side, I line them up with the Devil's head.

I let go before he sees.

He glances up, jerks his head to the side, and the yoked blocks tumble past his ear. They smash into the outstretched arm of the tower.

He straightens up and continues striding towards me. His voice hardens. "You can't go back. Ever. And you'll never see your wife again. I'll make sure of that."

From the distance, a gargantuan groan like a badly blown horn.

The Devil hasn't noticed but out on the horizon—above

his head in his orientation—the gate between heaven and hell is moving.

I cough behind my hand. "I wouldn't be so sure. Everyone has to keep a card up their sleeve, especially when dealing with the Devil, and it's only fair I advise you that you should call it a day, regroup, if you want to have any kind of army left."

"Ha! You do know who you're trying to bluff here?"

"Ah, but is it a bluff or a double bluff?" I lean out further. "I've nothing to lose, remember? Maybe you're prepared to gamble everything."

I point at the gate, clearly closing now, if—because of its colossal size—incredibly slowly.

The Devil halts, leans back, looks up. "What... When did you... How is that..."

"There's just time to make it through, if you hurry."

"Stop. Open it. Open the..." His arms are shooting out in every direction. "What do you think everyone here's going to do when they realize there's no one running the show?"

"Who said there wasn't?" I wave arm-over-arm at the helicopter, turn back to the Devil. "Go home. You're not needed. The position's already filled."

Closer already, he's staring straight at me. "What, who?" A pause. "You...?"

I shrug. "You really think I'd go to the trouble of killing Him just to have the mantle of godhead pass to you?"

"You didn't... You wouldn't..." But the energy's ebbed from his voice and I can tell he believes me.

"Well, let's face it, I can only do a better job than you." I point at the closing gate. "Better get going, while you still can."

He looks up at his screaming jets making giant U-turns in the sky, his gunship helicopters swinging around their tail booms to head back the way they've come.

On the ground, black tanks and troop carriers are already converging on the narrowing gap.

The Devil flings glances left and right, spots his

helicopter, carries on. He's got no choice. There's no way he can board it from the side of a building.

"You don't know how long this has taken..." My head does a little rebound on my neck because his mouth moves out of time with his voice, which comes as if from all around. "...and now you've ruined *everything*!" Although his mouth movements resync with his speech, his face contorts, horribly, into an animal-like leer.

He gallops up the side of the tower with, I swear, backwards-bending knees inside flapping trouser legs and the clack-clack of hooves.

The helicopter shoots upwards, roars to a halt just higher than the tower, tilts towards it.

I can't keep an eye on both, and the Devil's almost upon me. He raises a hoof as if to kick and I fall back, which is just as well because my eardrums pulsate to the helicopter's clattering. It's hurtling towards me too, coming in low, sideways over the roof.

It shoots over me in one plane and the Devil leaps in another, grabs a skid.

He hangs from it, one-handed, two-handed, still swinging as the helicopter whisks him away.

I push myself off the deck, get up.

His hooves dangle, pointing the way.

He's breathing hard. "I'll track you... With my panopticon... Come for you... Just when you think you're home and dry... Rip your limbs off one by one... Feed them to the dogs... Make you watch them poop you out..."

"I'll stay here, in your blind spot." I take out the bud of the earpiece.

I throw that and the stick microphone off the top of the tower.

Chapter 16

A Heavenly Glimpse of Earth

Hatch safely secured, I watch the last of the Devil's army whip through the vertical black fissure on the horizon like the tail of a stricken creature just before the hairline crack disappears as the gate shuts.

I turn away from the floor-to-ceiling window of the office.

About to pass the desk, I pause, head around the back of it and perch on the black swivel chair. Gripping the armrests makes my arms feel like they're floating. I lean back in the seat, sink into it, carry on sinking and eventually come to rest feeling like the rest of me is floating too. Already, I don't ever want to get up. I'm raising my feet to the edge of the desk when I glance at the terminal.

My feet clonk to the floor.

I lean forwards, type in "K-A-T-E- D-E-S-U-T-H-E" and hit "Search".

A couple of namesakes come up:

> Kate Desuthe, damned
>
> Kate Desuthe, saved
>
> Kate Desuthe... status pending

It looks like it might be possible to filter by job titles and earth dates but I'm not sure how and "Status pending" seems as good a definition of life as any, so I click on that.

The screens on the opposite wall come on. Colors

muted, each one's a mosaic of lighter and darker patches that move as one. Collectively, they make up a face. A slightly old-fashioned, heart-shaped face with a very small mouth.

Kate's. It's Kate's. My Kate's. My heart bounces around my chest as I jump up.

I blunder into the desk, sidestep around it, keep going.

I stop in front of the screen and she fills my vision.

Even stationary, I've the sensation of movement. Of pulling back, when that's the last thing I want to do.

It's arrested.

Her hands are clutched in front of her.

A bunch of pale roses sticks out.

Behind her, light fills the gaps between branches. The trees have dumped half their leaves. No wonder she's all wrapped up.

What happened to summer? Where did summer go?

A swivel and dip as she stoops changes the vantage point and rearranges the background. Trees and sky are replaced by darker earth tones. And stone. Lots of stone. Various sizes but mostly upright, row of slabs surmounts row of slabs.

The breeze catches and caresses her hair.

Leaning forwards, she places the roses at the foot of the nearest headstone.

So close that they stretch across two screens, I can make out my name and a pair of dates as etched into my memory as they are into stone. The first is the date I was born. The second is the date of the crash.

She's no idea how low I sank or how high I've risen since.

Maybe it's better that way.

She stands.

Back to her face. Yes...

She's pass-out pale, and her dark, soulful, sorrowful eyes glisten moistly out from under puffy lids, above lumpy-looking cheeks.

She's been crying, a lot, and a tiny world within a world starts its journey down her cheek now. No, no... "Kate, don't, please, I thought you were... We sort of swapped..." It feels as if something tears in my throat. I swallow. "So long as you're okay, that's all that matters." I press my hand to the glass. "And I'm going to make sure you are."

Her head jolts as if she's heard.

Her clear eyes are focused beyond me but the blood rushes through me. It's as if she's staring into mine.

"I understand now." I place my hand over her cheek. "We're slivers of love. Love is what we are. It permeates—"

A creak from the other room and my head jerks round.

The inner door's open.

I turn back to Kate, who's looking at me again but the other me this time—the one tucked up tight under the blanket of earth.

I edge towards the doorway.

Chapter 17

A Light That Shines Through Everything

I hasten my pace. The curtain shudders at my approach.

I tug the flaps apart.

Instantly I'm basking in waves of pure love that's warmer than sunshine and all-pervading. It shines through me.

I rest my elbows on the raised side of the bed and peer down at God, so small, so vulnerable. In His young but roly, rumpled skin, with His chubby arms and bandy baby legs, miniature feet and tiny balled hands, He lies on His back with His eyes closed. His snuffly breathing comes and goes. Is He dreaming? About us?

I reach in and, simultaneously bathed in light and inhaling His warm scent, gently pick Him up.

Shifting His weight further up one arm, I cradle Him with the crook of it supporting His overlarge head.

The total trust and innocence make hate impossible.

I'm putting God down when He opens the lustrous worlds of His eyes and gurgles.

"Yes," I say. "Yes. It's all going to be alright."

The Devil lied to me, so I lied to the Devil. I used his own tendency to believe in evil over goodness against him. If he hasn't already, soon he'll find out that his old— young—adversary is very much alive.

That'll teach him to mess with poets.

Chapter 18

Separation Anxiety

I head back through to the office and, like a helpless addict, I'm drawn to the screens.

Side on, Kate's crouching at my graveside.

She kisses the tips of the fingers of one hand and touches them to the earth.

No...

Pressing off from black-nyloned knees, she's getting up.

Don't go...

She's turning. Not yet...

Behind glass, she trudges away up the incline.

As the point of view swings a little, from one side of her departing back to the other, I spot a figure off to the side.

Leaning against a tombstone, he's got his head down.

When he raises it, he's smiling.

How... No!

It's the Dark Lord.

I knock on the glass. "Kate!"

I'm in danger of breaking it. "Kate! Kate!"

The Devil sets off after her, in a pair of shoes, with knees the right way around and hands clasped behind his back.

"Kate!"

She can't hear me.

"Kate!" I scream.

No wonder God's crying in the next room.

About the Author

Mark Kirkbride lives in England and is the author of two novels, *Satan's Fan Club* and *Game Changers of the Apocalypse*. His short stories can be found in *Under the Bed, Sci Phi Journal* and *Flash Fiction Magazine*. His poetry has appeared in the *Big Issue,* the *Morning Star*, the *Mirror* and Horror Writers Association chapbooks. His job as a subtitle editor in London means he is often in the odd position of having seen the book and read the film.

Printed in Great Britain
by Amazon